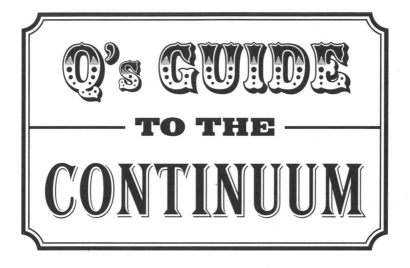

Q's GUIDE

TO THE

CONTINUUM

This book is a work of fiction. Names, characters, places and incidents are products of the authors' imagination or are used fictitiously. Any resemblance to actual events or locales or persons living or dead is entirely coincidental.

An *Original* Publication of POCKET BOOKS

POCKET BOOKS, a division of Simon & Schuster Inc.
1230 Avenue of the Americas, New York, NY 10020

STAR TREK is a Registered Trademark of Paramount Pictures.

This book is published by Pocket Books, a division of Simon & Schuster Inc., under exclusive license from Paramount Pictures.

ISBN: 0-671-01948-1

First Pocket Books paperback printing September 1998

10 9 8 7 6 5 4 3 2 1

POCKET and colophon are registered trademarks of Simon & Schuster Inc.

Printed in the U.S.A.

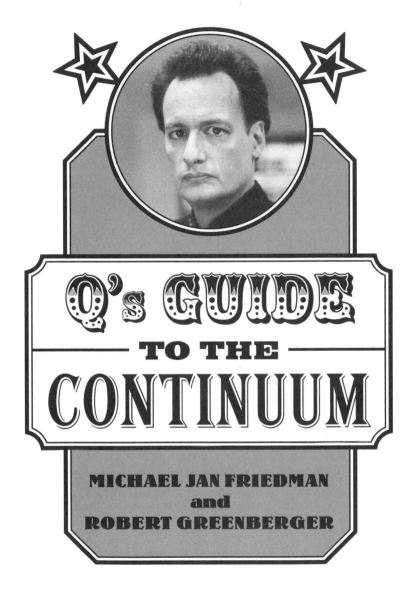

Q's GUIDE
— TO THE —
CONTINUUM

MICHAEL JAN FRIEDMAN
and
ROBERT GREENBERGER

NEW YORK   LONDON   TORONTO   SYDNEY   TOKYO   LONDON

A MESSAGE FROM Q

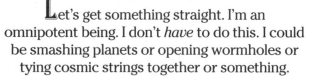

Let's get something straight. I'm an omnipotent being. I don't *have* to do this. I could be smashing planets or opening wormholes or tying cosmic strings together or something.

So listen closely. This isn't just another compendium of eclectic minutiae. This is the galaxy's most clever, insightful, and authoritative compendium of eclectic minutiae, as reported by someone who's been on hand for every event in every locale since the dawn of time— and then some.

You want to know who the longest-lived humanoids in the universe are? It's in here. You want to get the skinny on the galaxy's most devoted mother? That's in here too.

Curious about the greatest mass murderers in history? This is the place to look. In fact, any bit of lore that's not in this tome probably isn't worth knowing anyway.

No—not probably. *Definitely*.

So read on. If I were you, I'd get to know these nuggets of wisdom inside and out. I mean, you never know when someone will pop a quiz on you—with, say, the fate of the human race hanging in the balance.

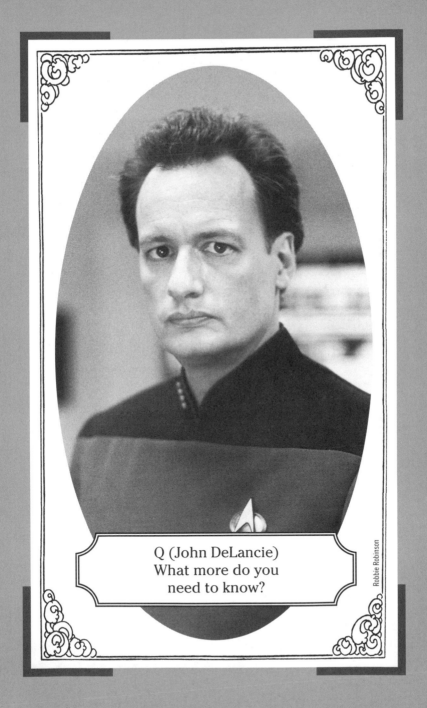

Q (John DeLancie)
What more do you
need to know?

Robbie Robinson

The Galaxy's LONGEST FEUD

The Lornaks and the Tralestas, two clans that originated on the planet Acamar III, had a bitter quarrel that lasted three centuries. Actually, it would have gone on even longer...except the Tralestas were eventually wiped out.
At that point, the feud became rather pointless, I suppose. It's no fun to squabble with someone unless they can squabble back.

!)?%(+*#!#*!)?%*(+*#!#*!)?%*(+*#!#*!)?%*(+*#

+)%¿(i*#i#*+)*%¿(i*#i#*+)*%¿(i*#i#*+)*%¿(i*

Sovereign Marouk (Nancy Parson) extends
the offer of peace to the Gatherer Brull (Joey Aresco).
Finally. The only thing ever known to have
taken longer was a ritual called "standing in line
at the DMV."

3

The Galaxy's
LARGEST Single-Celled ORGANISM

In 2268, a massive spaceborne organism composed of but a single cell made a meal of the Gamma 7A star system and then had the *U.S.S. Intrepid* for dessert. This creature strongly resembled the sort of microscopic protozoans one finds on certain life-bearing worlds... with the teensy difference that it was 18,000 kilometers long and 3,000 kilometers wide.

The organism was eventually destroyed by an antimatter bomb planted in its nucleus. *Ka-plooosh!*

Not the most appealing image in the universe, I'll grant you—but then, a lot of people don't think humanoids are so aesthetically pleasing either.

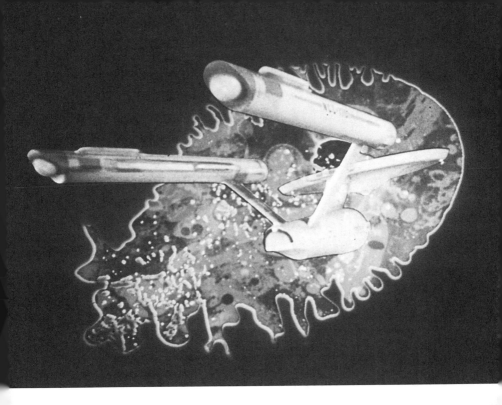

■

If you think this is big, think
of the size of the Petri dish.

■

The Galaxy's

Longest Continuous Avoidance

of

Admirals' Banquets

Jean-Luc Picard avoided going to these tedious affairs for six years in a row...preferring to attend to the tedious details of command on his vessel, the *U.S.S. Enterprise*, NCC-1701-D.

Go figure.

He looks like he's going to his own execution. Lighten up, Jean-Luc (Patrick Stewart).

THE GALAXY'S

MOST PAINFUL RITE OF PASSAGE

In the ritual known as the Age of Ascension, a Klingon warrior attains a new level of spiritual enlightenment by proclaiming, "Today I am a warrior. I must show you my heart. I travel the river of blood." Who comes up with this drivel?

Then the warrior walks between two lines of Klingons, who subject him or her to extreme agony via the use of painstiks. They also have the option of dragging their nails across a blackboard, though that's not talked about much.

And while his friends and family are torturing him within an inch of his life, the warrior is expected to express his or her innermost feelings.

No wonder Klingons don't smile.

That Worf (Michael Dorn) —
what a par-ty animal! He can
go ahead and take my turn.

9

The Galaxy's
MOST
Difficult
GAME

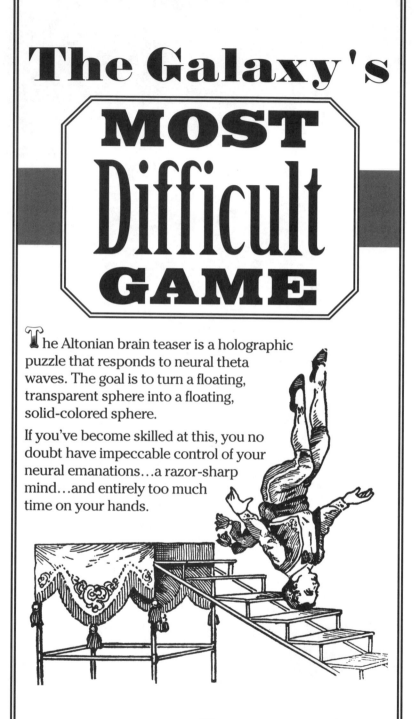

The Altonian brain teaser is a holographic puzzle that responds to neural theta waves. The goal is to turn a floating, transparent sphere into a floating, solid-colored sphere.

If you've become skilled at this, you no doubt have impeccable control of your neural emanations…a razor-sharp mind…and entirely too much time on your hands.

She's better with a *bat'leth*.

Surrounded by Vulcans all day
long. It would drive even a Q mad.

The Galaxy's

Most Patient Human Being

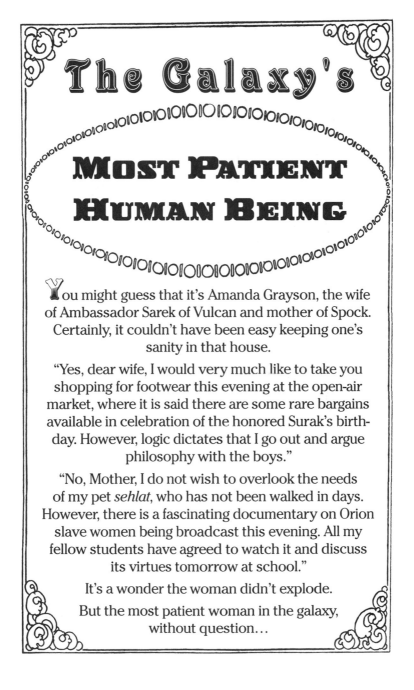

You might guess that it's Amanda Grayson, the wife of Ambassador Sarek of Vulcan and mother of Spock. Certainly, it couldn't have been easy keeping one's sanity in that house.

"Yes, dear wife, I would very much like to take you shopping for footwear this evening at the open-air market, where it is said there are some rare bargains available in celebration of the honored Surak's birthday. However, logic dictates that I go out and argue philosophy with the boys."

"No, Mother, I do not wish to overlook the needs of my pet *sehlat*, who has not been walked in days. However, there is a fascinating documentary on Orion slave women being broadcast this evening. All my fellow students have agreed to watch it and discuss its virtues tomorrow at school."

It's a wonder the woman didn't explode.

But the most patient woman in the galaxy, without question…

…is Yvette Gessard Picard.

After all, who else could have made
a semi-respectable adult out of such
a stubborn and ill-spirited child?
Dear lady, I salute you.

THE GALAXY'S

Best Way to Blow Up a Federation Starship

Listen closely—especially you Cardassians and such, who are always mixing it up with ships called *Enterprise, Excelsior, Endeavour, Exeter,* and *Excalibur* (don't those people know there are other letters in the alphabet?). I'm only going to say this once.

In a well-run warp drive propulsion system, magnetic seals and confinement fields prevent antimatter from touching the surface of the storage pod or any other part of the starship. When antimatter containment fails, what follows is a catastrophic malfunction—resulting in total destruction of the spacecraft.

Or in layman's terms...*whammo!*

Now get out there and blow up a few vessels. Make this omnipotent being proud.

Robbie Robinson

Isabella (Shay Astar) plots the destruction of the *Enterprise*. No wonder Jean-Luc hates children.

The Galaxy's

MOST UNPLEASANT

Imaginary Friend

In 2368, little Clara Sutter of the *Enterprise*-D found that her imaginary friend, Isabella, had suddenly come to life. Actually, "Isabella" was a nebula-dwelling life-form bent on draining the ship of its precious energy and dooming everyone on board.

And you thought *you* had problems.

Funny thing, though—the life-form took a liking to little Clara. When "Isabella" saw that she was hurting her human playmate, she decided to leave the *Enterprise* alone and find some other energy source to munch on.

Then again, now that I think about it, "Isabella" wasn't truly the most unpleasant imaginary friend in the galaxy. That honor is reserved for…

…the Gorgan, a noncorporeal life-form who reared his ugly head—and I do mean ugly—during James Kirk's stint on the *Enterprise*.

First, he drove the adult members of the Starnes Expedition to suicide on the planet Triacus. Then he deceived their children, including young Tommy Starnes, into thinking he was a "friendly angel" so they would follow him and do his evil bidding.

The children could summon the Gorgan by chanting, "Hail, hail, fire and snow. Call the Angel, we will go. Far away, for to see, Friendly Angel come to me." Droll, but effective—at least until Kirk opened the children's eyes and showed them the kind of low-life lunatic they were dealing with.

Obviously, the Gorgan was a rather poor choice of playmate for impressionable youngsters like Tommy Starnes and his friends. Or anyone else, for that matter.

How maudlin.
Who writes his material?

The Galaxy's
MOST PLEASANT
Imaginary Friend

One night, while strolling on the Promenade on that silly station of his, Benjamin Sisko met a lovely female named Fenna. The two fell in love. (Yawn.)

But Fenna wasn't a real woman at all. She was a psychoprojective alter ego composed of pure energy—the inadvertent creation of a telepath named Nidell, who was less than pleased with her home life.

Get it? Fenna, who looked exactly like Nidell, was out to find the happiness Nidell was denied. Unfortunately for Sisko, when Nidell's emotional problems were resolved, Fenna popped right out of existence.

Don't you just hate when that happens?

Robbie Robinson

Fenna (Salli Elise Richardson)…
or is it Nidell?

The GALAXY'S WORDIEST TREATY

The Treaty of Armens, established in 2255 between the Sheliak Corporate and the United Federation of Planets, cedes several Class-H Federation worlds to the Sheliak. (So what? I could cede a few worlds myself if I wanted to, and I wouldn't need a treaty to do it.)

Of slightly more interest is the fact that the treaty document contains half a million words and took 372 Federation legal experts to draft. Actually, with all those lawyers, the bill for services may have been longer than the treaty itself.

Lawyers. Pfah. You can't live with them and you can't eradicate them from every imaginable reality. On the other hand, it might be fun to try.

22

1290.D.1. Third Party Arrangements. Third party assistance may be requested from a Federation space vessel if the distance from the vessel to Sol Sector is greater than 5000 lightyears, UFP Standards Measurement Bureau units. Assistance may also be requested if the vessel is less than 1000 lightyears from a standard UFP subspace relay booster station.

1290.D.2 Third Party Arrangements, Cultural Contact Reference. See TA3508.D.1.g. A UFP crewmember from the Cultural Contact Office shall be on board a Galaxy-class Starfleet vessel at all times.

1290.D.3 Third Party Arrangements, Culture-of-Choice Decisions. When a Request for Assistance is implemented by the master of a Starfleet vessel, it shall be his/her decision as to the exact culture chosen to act as Arbiter. See TA 2343.K.7.d. The home planet for the Culture-of-Choice may reside at no greater distance from the requesting vessel than 2500 lightyears, UFP Standards Measurement Bureau units. If the Culture-of-Choice occupies one or more settlement worlds in the vicinity of the requesting vessel, a representative delegation may be culled from said worlds. See TA 8557.R.3.e.

1290.D.4 Transportation of Culture-of-Choice Delegates. The United Federation of Planets will nominally transport members of the delegation within the environment conditions of the Culture-of-Choice. Where this is not feasible or desired by the Culture-of-Choice, the delegation may arrange for indigenous vehicle transport or other party transport. In such cases, the UFP will reimburse the delegation for expenses, provided they are able to produce adequate receipts. The UFP will not consider a few incomprehensible numbers scrawled on the back of a cocktail napkin to be a valid receipt, even if it is considered to be the proper form of documentation on the delegates' home planet. We really must maintain some sense of bureaucracy.

583.7 Any Federation lawyer who thinks we're going to remember all this stuff must think we've got brains the size of a planet. Treaty violations, such as crash-landing on the Shellac planet should have been covered in the text of the treaty, or didn't anyone think about that eventuality when the bloody document was first drawn up?

583.8 Just one more paragraph until the critical one, where we talk about consultations, that kind of thing. The Shellacs don't sound like a race we ought to be selling planets to, if we have to write one of these contracts each time. Although, that's why we have computers, so we can do search-and-replace. Come to think about it, that's what the Shellac want to do with the colony on the planet.

LCARS SEARCH PARAMETERS EXECUTED: KEYWORDS CONSULTATION COM MODE DISPUTE QUERY REQUESTS

583.9 This section deals with the right of each party to confer with the other in the event something screwy happens with the treaty. This consultation may take the form of normal EM spectrum communication, subspace EM communication, or face-to-face meetings.
583.9.1 Normal EM radio communication may be achieved over a set of frequencies prescribed in the Appendix. There's that pesky organ again.

583.9.2 Subspace frequencies are likewise prescribed in the Appendix. You might have to look carefully for them.
They're slippery little devils. Subspace communication is not recommended when both parties are in normal reference space-time, unless a truly secured channel is desired.

583.9.3 Face-to-face meetings are recommended when both parties actually have faces. In those instances when one party possesses only a body and tail, it will be refered to as a face-to-tail

It makes you wonder if anyone has really read
this whole treaty. In case you're interested,
I wrote clause 1290.D.4.

The Most
FUTILE
CAMPAIGN
TO SEIZE CONTROL
of a
GOVERNMENT

Once upon a time, there were two Klingon sisters named Lursa and B'Etor, whose big brother Duras was a muckety-muck on the Klingon High Council. Following Duras's untimely death in 2367, the sisters fell from favor.

This made them angry—so angry, in fact, that they conspired with the hated Romulans to make Duras's idiot son leader of the council. The result? A bold and bloody civil war as only the Klingons know how to wage one. In the end, the sisters' forces were thrashed. Lursa and B'Etor themselves were lucky to escape with their cleavages intact.

Two years later, the sisters surfaced again, attempting to raise capital for new armies by selling bilitrium explosives to a Bajoran terrorist on Deep Space 9. And still later, they illegally mined a magnesite deposit on Kalla III in the hope of peddling the ore to the Yridians.

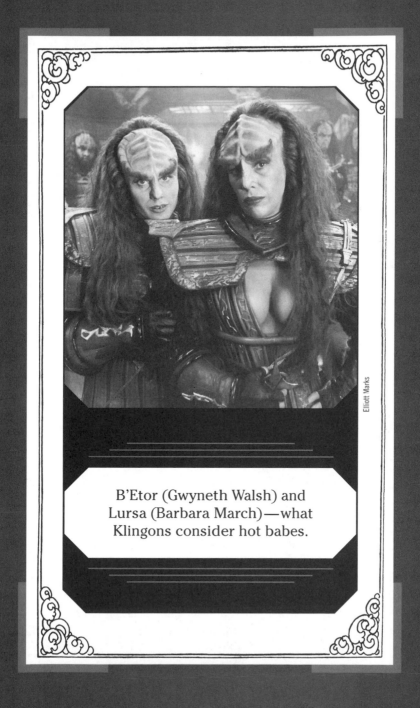

B'Etor (Gwyneth Walsh) and Lursa (Barbara March)—what Klingons consider hot babes.

Elliott Marks

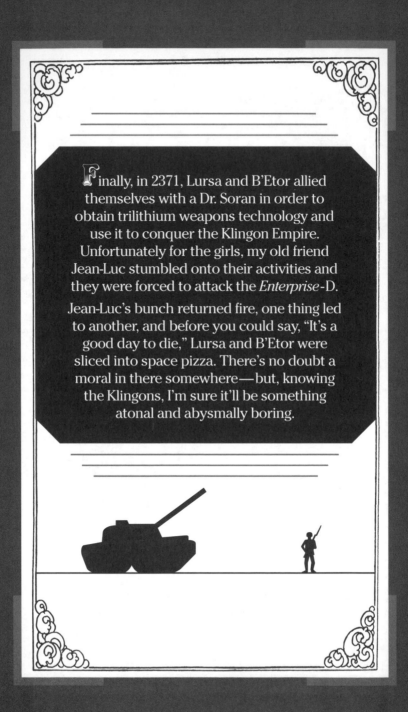

inally, in 2371, Lursa and B'Etor allied themselves with a Dr. Soran in order to obtain trilithium weapons technology and use it to conquer the Klingon Empire. Unfortunately for the girls, my old friend Jean-Luc stumbled onto their activities and they were forced to attack the *Enterprise*-D.

Jean-Luc's bunch returned fire, one thing led to another, and before you could say, "It's a good day to die," Lursa and B'Etor were sliced into space pizza. There's no doubt a moral in there somewhere—but, knowing the Klingons, I'm sure it'll be something atonal and abysmally boring.

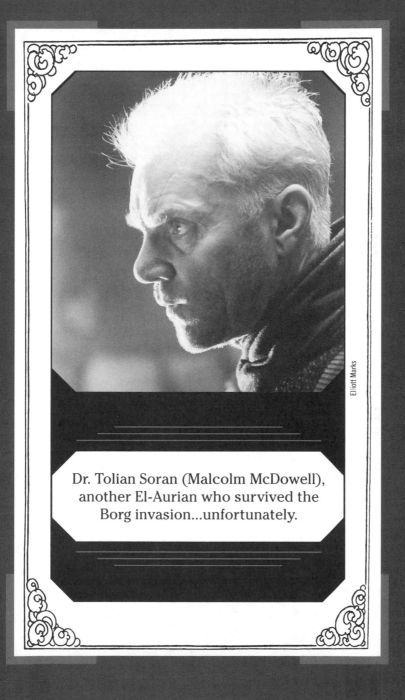

Dr. Tolian Soran (Malcolm McDowell), another El-Aurian who survived the Borg invasion...unfortunately.

Elliott Marks

The Galaxy's
LAZIEST SPACE TRAVELERS

The Cytherians, who reside on a world near the center of the galaxy, could have ventured out into space like everyone else. But no— they had to be different.

Instead of boldly going out to meet other races, the Cytherians sit on their rotund posteriors and bring other races to them. How do they accomplish this, you ask? They send out special probes designed to take control of spaceship computers.

All in all, a rather stupid approach, if you ask me—and even if you don't. I mean, boldly waiting for other people to come to you? Where's the fun in that?

THE GALAXY'S LONGEST RITUAL FOR SAYING HELLO

When the natives of the planet Chandra V meet each other on the street, it takes them three days to greet one another.

Obviously, they have immensely strong bladders.

The Longest Time Spent Trapped in a Temporal Causality Loop

That title goes to the *U.S.S. Bozeman,* hands down.

Under the command of Captain Morgan Bateson, who was obviously a couple of photons short of a torpedo (if you catch my drift), the *Soyuz*-class ship left its home starbase in 2278. Three weeks later, the *Bozeman* disappeared near the Typhon Expanse—and remained there until 2368, a span of (get this) ninety years.

During those nine decades, the crew of the *Bozeman* didn't know all that time was going by. You see, they were caught in a recursive temporal causality loop, which caused them to experience the same few events over and over and over and over…

…like a broken record, until the loop was mercifully disrupted by the *Enterprise*-D.

Something similar happened to me once. I hiccoughed and missed the creation of life on Vulcan. But then, I'm told I didn't really miss *much*.

Captain Morgan Bateson (Kelsey Grammer),
a man ripped from his own time and plunked
down a century later. Could be worse. He
could have spent a couple of hours trapped
with Beverly Crusher.

The Galaxy's
Most Brutal
DENTAL PRACTICE

~ ~ ~ ~ ~ ~ ~ ~ ~ ~ ~ ~ ~ ~

Cardassian citizens all have a molar extracted at age ten so the Cardassian bureau of identification can keep them on file. This was discovered by Deep Space 9's Chief Miles O'Brien when he was tried on Cardassia Prime for a crime he didn't commit.

Sounds like a cruel practice, doesn't it? But then, O'Brien had sat through Benjamin Sisko's weekly briefing sessions. By comparison, the tooth extraction must have seemed like a walk in the park.

Now rinse your mouth out and spit.

O'Brien (Colm Meaney) finds it is not the hand of friendship that is being extended to him.

THE GALAXY'S
BEST EXAMPLE
of
PEACEFUL COEXISTENCE

The Carraya System, located near the Romulan-Klingon border, is host to a secret Romulan prison camp. Established several months after the infamous Khitomer massacre of 2346, it houses nearly a hundred Klingon warriors who were captured from a perimeter outpost near Khitomer.

Naturally, the Romulan government wanted to execute the warriors—probably not a bad idea at the time. However, a Romulan officer named Tokath, in a magnanimous but incredibly ill-considered gesture, sacrificed his military career to establish a home for his prisoners.

In the years that followed, a peaceful coexistence developed between Romulan jailer and Klingon captive—so peaceful, in fact, that Tokath even took a Klingon woman as his wife, bumpy forehead and all.

All right, so it's not exactly the stuff of epic poetry. Still, you've got to admit—if Klingons and Romulans can live together in harmony, there may be hope for the rest of you drooling mortals.

Robbie Robinson

Tokath (Alan Scarfe) hoists a
drink to good fellowship.
Why can't we all just get along?

35

The Silliest EXAMPLE of Interspecies COOPERATION

A barely habitable world in the Neutral Zone, Nimbus III became the site of a "bold" experiment in 2268 when the Federation, the Romulans, and the Klingons established a joint settlement there. Dubbed the "planet of galactic peace," Nimbus III was to be the first place in the universe where all three species were welcome.

At least, that was the nonsense the Klingon High Council, the Romulan Senate, and the Federation president were spouting at the time. But you know how smart they are.

Needless to say, the plan turned out to be a dismal failure.

However, the settlement itself remained in place as a haven for smugglers, thieves, and cutthroats for some twenty years thereafter, so maybe it wasn't a complete waste of time.

Ah, just look at the happy natives living in peace and harmony—and so eager to ram it down each other's throats.

THE GALAXY'S
Most
Practical
DIVORCE
REQUIREMENTS

When a Klingon female
wishes to divorce her mate,
she simply declares
"N'Gos tlhogh cha!"
Translation:
"Our marriage is done!"

Oh, and then she belts
him in the mouth.
And spits on him.

Come to think of it,
this may not be
for everyone.

Robbie Robinson

Grilka
(Mary Kay Adams),
a typical Klingon
female—wondering
what your head would
look like on the point
of a *bat'leth*.

THE GALAXY'S SPEEDIEST LOVE AFFAIR

Early in the twenty-third century, the Scalosians were biochemically hyper-accelerated by volcanic radiation. In layman's terms, they sped up their bodily processes to the point where they couldn't even be seen by other humanoids.

The radiation also decreased fertility in Scalosian females and completely sterilized all Scalosian males. This was not a good portent for future generations.

To preserve their species, the Scalosians were forced to mate outside it. In effect, they set up a cosmic dating service—sending distress calls to passing space-ships and hyperaccelerating the crews, then arranging trysts between male crewmen and Scalosian females.

Boy...talk about your "quickies."

THE GALAXY'S

MOST IMPRESSIVE

SPORTS RECORD

In 1941, a baseball player named Joe DiMaggio scored something called a "hit" in fifty-six consecutive games. The feat remained unequaled for eighty-five years until it was eclipsed by Harmon "Buck" Bokai, a shortstop for the London Kings.

I am not what one might call a baseball aficionado. However, Benjamin Sisko is, and he says DiMaggio's hitting streak was considered the one sports record that would never be broken.

Sorry, Joe. Better luck in some alternative reality.

The Worst
ROOMMATE
for
ETERNITY

In 2267, a scientist named Lazarus created a passageway to an antimatter universe. The existence of this passageway posed a rather grave peril. After all, even the slightest contact between the two continua (the plural of continuum—eloquent, aren't I?) would result in the total annihilation of both universes.

Not that it mattered to me, personally. But if I were a limited, mortal being in one of those two universes, it would have mattered a lot.

To make the situation even worse, Lazarus was completely insane. He believed that his alternate self from the other universe wanted to kill him.

Fortunately, the alternate Lazarus was a bit more stable. Noting the danger posed by his counterpart, he met the poor, deluded fellow in the interdimensional corridor and left orders to seal it up with both of them inside.

As a result, both universes were made safe…but only at the cost of a significant personal sacrifice. The sane Lazarus is now forced to wrestle with his fruitcake of a twin for the rest of eternity.

But don't feel bad for him. Eternity isn't nearly as long as people seem to think.

Sane, but in desperate need of a shave.

THE GALAXY'S MOST DEVIOUS TAILOR

Elim Garak was one of the more ruthless agents in the Cardassian Obsidian Order until he was exiled to a space station known as Terok Nor. While in exile, Garak opened a clothing shop on the station's Promenade and went to work as a tailor.

He still operates that shop, even though the Federation has assumed control of the station and renamed it Deep Space 9. And he'll tell you that he's just a simple tailor—but don't believe it. As conniving and ruthless as ever, Garak gets his hands on more strategic information than any ten Cardassian legates combined.

Also, he charges like a bandit for alterations.

Garak (Andrew Robinson), just as dangerous with a sewing needle as with a phaser—maybe more so.

Robbie Robinson

The Galaxy's MOST EFFECTIVE CRYING JAG

James Kirk was bringing Elaan, the Dohlman of the planet Elas, to the planet Troyius. The Dohlman, an attractive woman by any standard—even mine—was slated to marry the ruler of Troyius and bring peace to their two warring worlds.

As luck would have it, the Dohlman wasn't thrilled by the idea. She broke down in front of Kirk, knowing his masculine instincts would spur him to dry her tears— which happened to contain the biochemical equivalent of a rather potent love potion.

Not that Kirk ever needed an excuse to act on his hormonal impulses. But thanks to Elaan's tears, he fell head over heels for her—and in doing so, jeopardized the Dohlman's marriage as well as the truce.

Fortunately, Kirk decided that he was more attracted to his ship than he was to Elaan, and the jilted Dohlman opted to move on to Troyius.

The Galaxy's Biggest Troublemakers

Redjac was an energy-based life-form that terrorized and murdered females throughout the galaxy, feeding on their fear.

On Deneb II, it was known as Kesla. On Rigel IV, it was known as Beratis. On Vulcan, it was known as "an energy-based life-form that terrorizes and murders females throughout the galaxy."

On Earth, it was known as…(spooky music)…Jack the Ripper.

In the twenty-third century, Redjac took the form of a man named Hengist and traveled to Argelius II, where it sliced and diced at least three more unsuspecting females. When the entity's true nature was discovered by Jim Kirk, it was transported into space…where it dispersed ever so harmlessly….

Or so you'd like to think (bwah-ha-ha).

However, as red-handed as Redjac was, there was an even bigger nuisance running around in the twenty-third century, the one we coyly refer to as the Beta XII-A entity.

An energy-based life-form like Redjac, it thrived on not just fear, but all negative emotions. Also, it was capable of manipulating matter as well as the minds of its victims in order to achieve its grisly ends.

My kind of guy.

In 2268, the Beta XII-A entity unleashed a squad of Klingon marauders on the crew of Jim Kirk's *Enterprise.* As these long-time enemies hacked each other's guts apart strand by strand, the entity gorged itself on their anger like a Ferengi at a Tube Grub Festival.

It was finally defeated by an act of peaceful cooperation between the Klingons and the *Enterprise* crew. That is to say, they got together and laughed at it.

Put off by their peculiar sense of humor, the entity packed its bags and got the hell out of there.

The Most Time SPENT IN A FEDERATION TRANSPORTER

Montgomery Scott, chief engineer aboard the original *Enterprise*, was relocating to a retirement colony when his transport vessel crashed onto the surface of a Dyson Sphere. Scott, one of two survivors of the crash, endured for seventy-five years by suspending his molecules in a transporter loop. (The other fellow didn't make it.)

No, I probably wouldn't have thought of that, either. But then, this was the same Montgomery Scott who routinely saved Jim Kirk's hindquarters in pinch after deadly pinch.

And they call *me* a miracle worker.

Quick, Scotty (James Doohan), go back! Before Jean-Luc can bore you with one of his *Stargazer* stories.

Robbie Robinson

The Galaxy's
MOST DEVOTED
MOTHER

♥

The Horta is a silicon-based life-form that resides on the planet Janus VI. Every fifty thousand years or so, all but one Horta dies, leaving the survivor to care for the species's entire brood in the quaintly named Vault of Tomorrow.

Do you know what it's like getting all those kids up in the morning? Or convincing them to clean up their Vault?

And potty-training? Don't ask.

There's no Mother's Day on Janus VI, but there ought to be. Of course, that would only present Momma Horta with another problem—how to find room for all those cards on her refrigerator.

The Horta and her progeny.
Obviously, they take after
their father.

THE GALAXY'S
LEAST LIKABLE
HUMANOID

Get a good look at her. Horrible, isn't she?

We met a couple of hundred years ago, but I'd rather not talk about it. In fact, I'd be personally indebted if you would just turn the page.

THE GALAXY'S MOST Aesthetically Pleasing TRANSFORMATION

Back in 2268, James Kirk and his cohorts found the *U.S.S. Exeter* orbiting the planet Omega IV, its entire crew reduced to a scattering of dehydrated crystals.

It's not that I find the crystal form particularly enchanting, but when you compare it to the *human* form...
Well, I think you get the picture.

Come on, man, pull yourself together. One little virus and these humans go all to pieces.

The Galaxy's
MOST
FREQUENTLY
CONQUERED
RACE

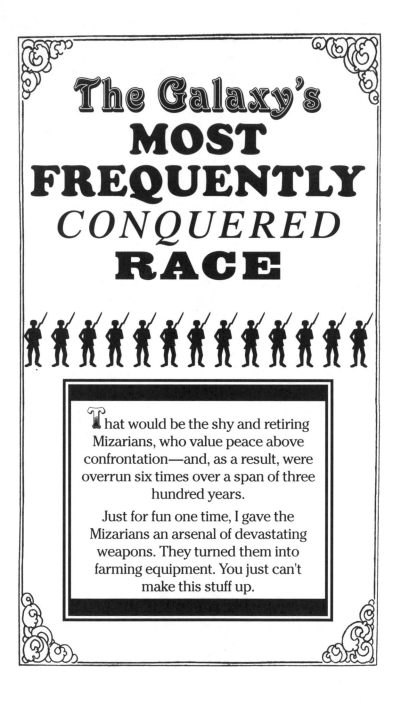

That would be the shy and retiring Mizarians, who value peace above confrontation—and, as a result, were overrun six times over a span of three hundred years.

Just for fun one time, I gave the Mizarians an arsenal of devastating weapons. They turned them into farming equipment. You just can't make this stuff up.

The Galaxy's
WISEST
Compilation of
Behavioral Directives
MASQUERADING
as a
PERSONALITY QUIRK

Ensign Robin Lefler of the *Enterprise*-D lived by a set of 102 colloquialisms she had collected. Law 17 was, "When all else fails, do it yourself." Law 46 was, "Life isn't always fair." And Law 91 was, "Always watch your back."

Though Ensign Lefler is unaware of it, her precepts are virtually identical to the Code of Ri'brahim, compiled by a highly intelligent and insightful Delta Quadrant race over the span of ten millennia.

Then again, you've heard the one about the monkeys and Shakespeare.

THE GALAXY'S BIGGEST BOO-BOO!

Richard Daystrom, a twenty-third-century computer scientist, won several pretentious awards at the age of twenty-four for his invention of duotronics—which became the basis for starship computer systems.

Unfortunately for Daystrom, he spent the rest of his life trying to live up to his reputation as a "boy wonder" and developed a few personality quirks as a result. Okay, maybe more than a few.

In the 2260s, Daystrom developed a system called multitronics, which imprinted neural engrams on computer circuitry—an attempt to enable a starship computer to think and reason like a human being.

That would have been a mistake in any case, since humans are a lot better at things like starting wars and procreating than thinking and reasoning. It became even worse when Daystrom used his own personality as a template.

The result? A war-games massacre in which nearly five hundred Starfleet personnel were obliterated and Daystrom himself went insane.

Sounds like a boo-boo to me.

A prime example of the fine line
between insanity and genius.
Unfortunately, he crossed the
line once too often.

John Gill, a prominent Federation historian, conducted a little "cultural experiment" on the planet Ekos in the mid-twenty-third century. To give the locals a more efficient form of government, Gill came up with one based on a regime that prevailed in Earth's past.

We're talking black uniforms with silver trim—very haute couture, though those who wore them had the moral fiber of a squash. Racial hatred, wholesale slaughter, a list of atrocities as long as your arm…what was it called again?

Oh yes. Nazi Germany.

Eventually, Gill's experiment took the same evil turn as the society it was modeled after. No surprise there, eh? A great many natives of the neighboring planet Zeon were imprisoned and killed, and eventually, even Gill lost his life.

I guess you'd have to call that an even bigger boo-boo.

The people of the planet Minos, who peddled the galaxy's most powerful weapons to whoever could pay for them, cheerfully nicknamed their world the "Arsenal of Freedom." One of their slogans was "Peace Through Superior Firepower."

The Minosians even practiced what they preached, installing an automated defense system—one which eventually backfired and annihilated every last sentient on their planet.

Now, that would have to be the *biggest* boo-boo of all.

The Galaxy's
ＭＯＳＴ ＵＮＣＥＲＴＡＩＮ
REAL ESTATE
INVESTMENT

A strange little planet named Meridian goes through a series of dimensional shifts every sixty years, causing both the world and its inhabitants to phase into and out of a corporeal state.

Now, if only I could convince *Riker* to take up residence there…

Robbie Robinson

Imagine being asleep for
sixty years and the first
thing you want do is eat.
You humanoids really *are*
dullards, aren't you?

THE GALAXY'S
Longest Dog Sitting
ASSIGNMENT

When Kathy Janeway took off for the Badlands in search of her humorless Vulcan security officer, she left her pal Mark on Earth with her pregnant Irish setter. Mark, a good-natured slob if ever I saw one, promised to take care of the animal and its progeny.

Then Kathy and her crew were cast into the Delta Quadrant, from whence she estimated it would take several decades to get home. In fact, Mark was forced to watch those dogs for...

Well, let's just say "a long time" and leave it at that. Anything more specific and I'd be telling, wouldn't I?

64

For this you turn down a Q?
Oh, Kathy…

The Most
OPPORTUNITIES FOR
ADVANCEMENT
DECLINED BY
A SINGLE
STARFLEET
OFFICER

Over a span of three years, a certain buffoonish individual who shall go unnamed (but whose initials are William T. Riker) turned down the captaincies of the *U.S.S. Drake,* the *U.S.S. Aries,* and the *U.S.S. Melbourne*—not to mention a level of power equal to my own.

And all to remain first officer of the *Enterprise*-D. It boggles even the most omniscient mind.

Carpe diem, already!

Robbie Robinson

The Species
MOST IN NEED
of
ORGAN DONORS

Two thousand years ago, the Vidiians were stricken by an illness called the phage, which gradually ate away the organs of their bodies. These people have survived only through the widespread use of organ transplantation to replace their diseased and—let's face it—rather disgusting body parts.

It's a fate I wouldn't wish on my worst enemy. Well, perhaps my very worst enemy. All right, maybe several of my worst enemies.

But when you think about it, who's worse off? The Vidiians—or their living, breathing organ donors, who often stop living and breathing once they make their "donations"?

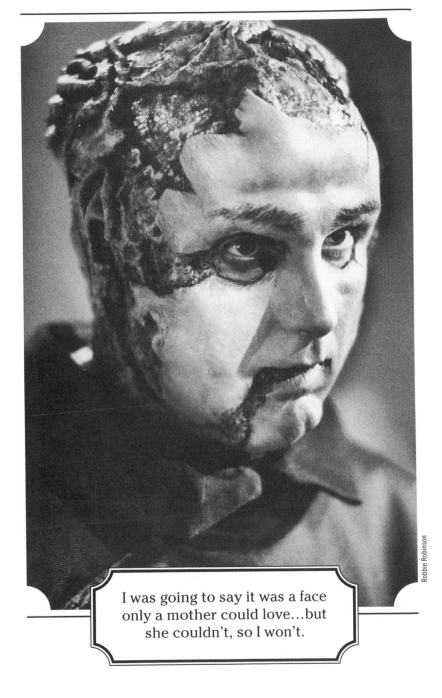

I was going to say it was a face
only a mother could love…but
she couldn't, so I won't.

The Galaxy's

MOST APT

DESCRIPTION

of the

HUMAN ANATOMY

The crystalline microbrains of Velara III once described the human crew members of the *Enterprise*-D as "ugly bags of mostly water."

The phrase is not only apt, it's accurate. After all, more than 90 percent of the molecules in the human body are composed of H_2O.

The other 10 percent, of course, is noxious gases.

THE GALAXY'S
Least Harmonious

WORK OF MUSIC

Alba Ra was a twenty-fourth–century music form developed by the Talarians. Electronic, discordant, and very loud, it was a favorite of Jono—a human raised by the Talarians, whom Captain Picard briefly took under his wing. Predictably, my friend Jean-Luc was…how shall I put it…not *fond* of *Alba Ra*.

However, *Alba Ra* is only a runner-up in this category. The truly least harmonious work of music…

…is *Aktuh and Melota*, a Klingon opera.

For those of you unfamiliar with the piece, *Aktuh and Melota* is a classic story of star-crossed lovers. Aktuh is the son of a powerful warlord; Melota, the daughter of a rival warlord. You see the problem.

After a savage and bloody tryst in which bones are broken and both participants are lucky to come away with their lives, Aktuh and Melota pledge their troth. This, despite the fact that their fathers would rather disembowel each other than sit together at a wedding feast.

(In point of fact, most Klingons seem ready to disembowel each other at the drop of a hat. But that's another matter entirely.)

Eventually, Aktuh's father gets wind of the courtship (literally, it seems) and decides to annihilate Melota's entire clan—Melota included—rather than permit such a disgrace. However, Aktuh can't allow anyone—including his father—to lift a blade against his betrothed.

What happens next is unnecessarily confusing. Before it's over, everyone's dead—Aktuh, Melota, their fathers, and several dozen supporting characters, as well as a number of people who appear to have no business being on stage in the first place.

Lieutenant Commander Worf on Deep Space 9 just *adores Aktuh and Melota*. But then, his idea of eloquence is a prolonged snarl.

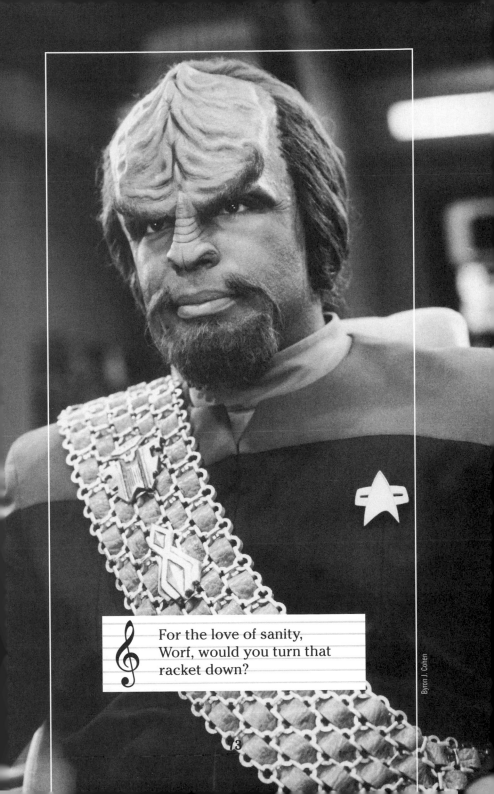

For the love of sanity, Worf, would you turn that racket down?

13

THE GALAXY'S MOST Long-Winded NEGOTIATION

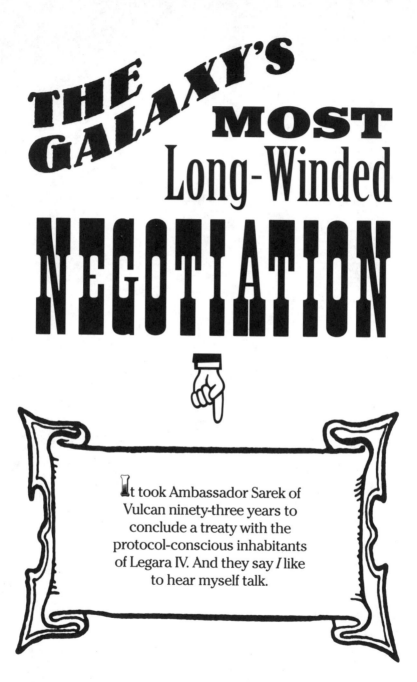

It took Ambassador Sarek of Vulcan ninety-three years to conclude a treaty with the protocol-conscious inhabitants of Legara IV. And they say *I* like to hear myself talk.

Robbie Robinson.

Do you know what's more boring than a Vulcan ambassador? Neither do I.

75

The Galaxy's WORST VACATION SPOT

Rura Penthe, a frozen, almost uninhabitable planetoid, was once the site of a Klingon prison camp known as the "aliens' graveyard"—largely because prisoners were worked to death in the dilithium mines there.

Of course, that wasn't the worst of it. The food was salty, the sheets too full of starch, and subspace transmissions from loved ones sometimes took days to arrive.

And the lack of courtesy from one's fellow prisoners…just don't get me started.

The good
Captain Kirk
(William Shatner) and
his fellow traveler,
Dr. McCoy (DeForest Kelley)
are shown to their luxurious
accommodations.
Mind the bodies.

77

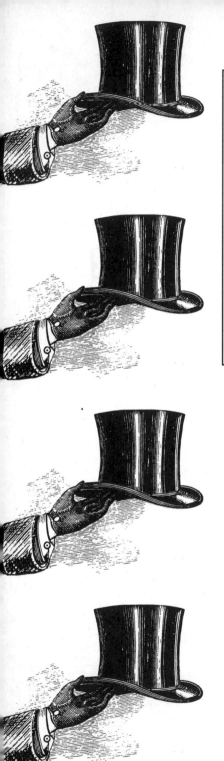

The Galaxy's MOST OBNOXIOUS REDUNDANCY

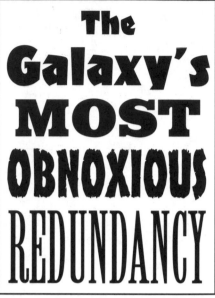

In 2361, a transporter accident created an exact duplicate of Will Riker. One copy of him returned safely to the *U.S.S. Potemkin*, where he continued his career as a junior officer. The other copy materialized back on the surface of Nervala IV.

The existence of the duplicate Riker wasn't discovered until eight years later (whoops). Once rescued, this Riker decided to use his middle name, Tom, to distinguish himself from his copy.

Now we have *two* Rikers. If you ask me, even *one* was two too many.

You know, eight years was not long enough. They should have left him there permanently. In fact they should have left them *both* there.

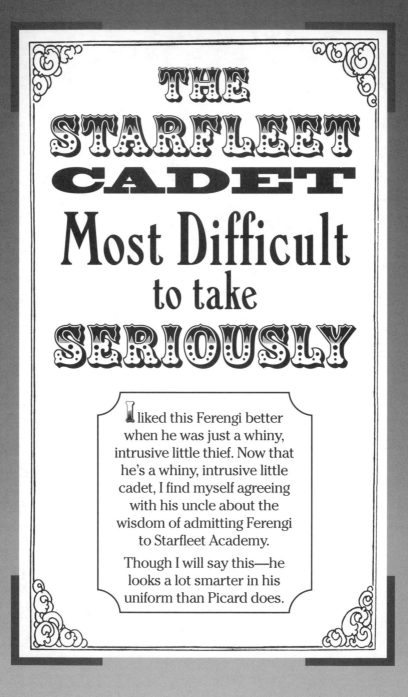

THE STARFLEET CADET

Most Difficult
to take
SERIOUSLY

I liked this Ferengi better when he was just a whiny, intrusive little thief. Now that he's a whiny, intrusive little cadet, I find myself agreeing with his uncle about the wisdom of admitting Ferengi to Starfleet Academy.

Though I will say this—he looks a lot smarter in his uniform than Picard does.

Given enough time, I bet he could be just as stuffy as Jean-Luc.

Robbie Robinson

The Galaxy's BIGGEST LIVING KLINGON

His name is Koral.
He smuggles things.
If I weren't so omnipotent,
even I would be scared
of him.

When you've said, Koral (James Worthy), you've said it tall.

Robbie Robinson

The Life-Form
LEAST LIKELY
TO SUBSIST
on a
LOW-SODIUM
DIET

In 2266, James Kirk ran into the last specimen of a species native to the planet M-113. Using its hypnotic ability to appear as someone else, the creature killed four members of Kirk's crew and a colonist named Crater…all to obtain the sodium chloride in their bodies.

And they say *humans* are dumb. Tell me this creature never heard of a saltshaker.

I could say it was a sucker for humans,
but as Q I'm above such puns.

The Galaxy's

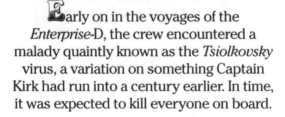

MOST AMUSING DISEASE

$\mathbb{E}$arly on in the voyages of the *Enterprise*-D, the crew encountered a malady quaintly known as the *Tsiolkovsky* virus, a variation on something Captain Kirk had run into a century earlier. In time, it was expected to kill everyone on board.

But first, it made them intoxicated and mentally unstable—that is, even more mentally unstable than usual—and, in some cases, strangely determined to engage in sexual behavior.

I don't suppose Picard and his people found the virus very funny, but I'm splitting a gut just thinking about it.

The Galaxy's
LEAST
PRODUCTIVE
TRIP

Some time ago, a Kelvan expedition made the voyage from its home in the Andromeda Galaxy to the Milky Way with an eye to colonization and conquest. And yet, by 2268, the expedition agreed to instead colonize a single planet.

Peaceably, no less. Talk about your diminished expectations.

THE GALAXY'S LONGEST MISSION of Exploration

The Klingon vessel *T'Ong* took off on a mission of exploration in the latter part of the twenty-third century and returned in 2365—seventy-five years later.

Obviously, Klingons don't like to ask for directions, either.

Of course, when the *T'Ong* left Klingon space, the Federation and the empire were still smiting each other pretty good and pretty often. Imagine the surprise on the hairy faces of the *T'Ong*'s crew when they saw Klingons on the bridge of the *Enterprise*-D.

Even then, the situation might have gotten ugly (a word one is legally bound to use liberally when referring to a certain bumpy-headed species). After all, Klingon captains are trained to be suspicious as well as guttural.

But before the Klingons on the *T'Ong* could get wild, Picard's tame ones talked them to death.

The Galaxy's MOST BIZARRE Death Ritual

In Ferengi society, mourners honor the dead by vacuum-desiccating their bodies, sealing them into disk-shaped souvenir containers, and then selling them to the highest bidder. If the deceased is a person of note, these containers can become valuable collector's items.

So when a Ferengi asks if he can "give you a hand," be advised—it may be his uncle Kluug's.

89

The Galaxy's
MOST INTRUSIVE
Time-Traveling
Person, Entity, Species, or Organization

(That is, besides yours truly.)

Where do I begin? Perhaps with the people who created the Guardian of Forever more than five billion years ago.

Originally, the Guardian was a waste-disposal system. After all, its creators didn't want to fill their own era with garbage, so they invented a way to send it to other eras.

Makes sense, doesn't it? The problem is, some species—some rather *primitive* species, I might add—occasionally saw the Guardian as a means of sending themselves through time.

Rather silly, actually. But then, you know what they say—one person's landfill is another person's treasure trove.

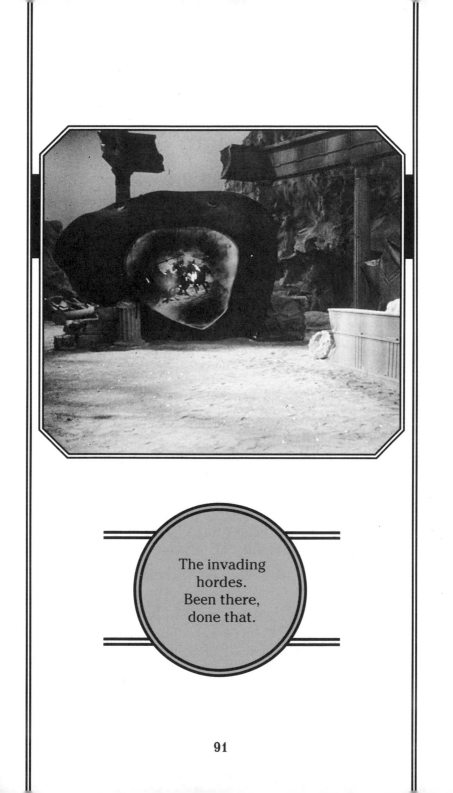

The invading
hordes.
Been there,
done that.

Slightly less benign were Ajur and Boratus, two twenty-seventh–century Vorgon criminals. These yutzes traveled back in time some three hundred years to obtain a quantum phase inhibitor invented by their contemporary, a scientist named Kal Dano.

You would think three hundred years of hindsight would have given these dastardly villains some edge...some small leg up...some itsy-bitsy advantage in their dealings with the denizens of the twenty-fourth century.

But no.

Ajur and Boratus were foiled by my friend Jean-Luc—hardly a rocket scientist in his own right—who, with the help of a lovely human female named Vash, destroyed the quantum phase inhibitor "to keep it from falling into the wrong hands."

Trust me on this—these two wouldn't have been a threat even *with* the device. In almost every timeline where they snatch the quantum phase inhibitor, they blow themselves up with it.

And in the few where they don't, they blow up Riker, which is nearly as good.

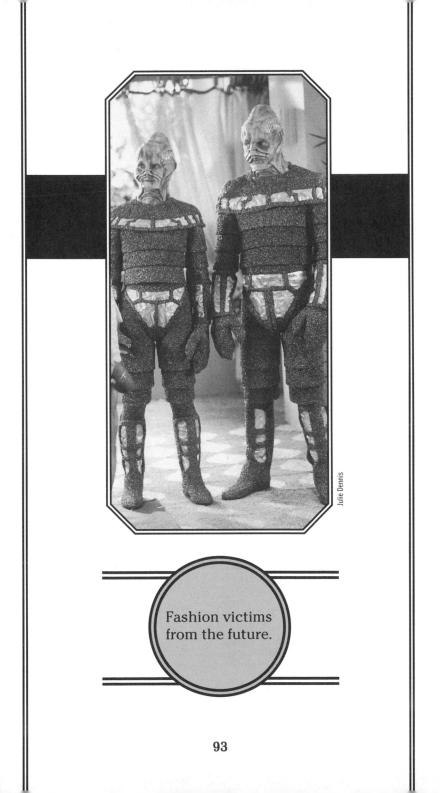

Julie Dennis

Fashion victims
from the future.

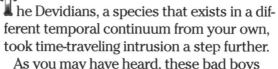

The Devidians, a species that exists in a different temporal continuum from your own, took time-traveling intrusion a step further. As you may have heard, these bad boys thrive on neural energy—the kind that exists in all living creatures....

Even Worf.

To get a heaping helping of the stuff, they sent an expedition to your continuum's nineteenth-century San Francisco—where they tried to extract neural energy galore from the multitudinous victims of a cholera epidemic.

Interesting plan, wouldn't you say? Fortunately for nineteenth-century San Francisco, my bosom buddy Jean-Luc stopped the Devidians, just as he stopped Ajur and Boratus.

Otherwise, they might have purloined neural energy from a great many other temporal junctures where people are sick to the point of death—any Friday night in Neelix's mess hall, for instance.

Nice try, Devidians. But I just can't find it in my heart to give you best-of-category.

My pick for most intrusive time travelers goes to a group that's been playing with history as if it were a twentieth-century pinball game…the inhabitants of a farflung world who took a bunch of Earthmen six thousand years ago and trained them and their ancestors to not only use table forks and balance their checkbooks, but also to intercede at crucial junctions in the timeline.

These expatriated humans operated in secret all up and down the temporal continuum until one of them—Supervisor 194, also known as Gary Seven—ran into Jim Kirk and the original *Enterprise* in the year 1968.

His mission? To help mankind survive its nuclear age. How successful was he in carrying it out?

Well…you're still alive, aren't you?

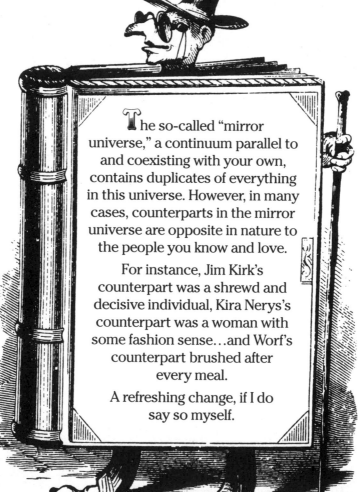

THE GALAXY'S
MOST INTERESTING
ALTERNATE REALITY

ALTERNATE REALITY

The so-called "mirror universe," a continuum parallel to and coexisting with your own, contains duplicates of everything in this universe. However, in many cases, counterparts in the mirror universe are opposite in nature to the people you know and love.

For instance, Jim Kirk's counterpart was a shrewd and decisive individual, Kira Nerys's counterpart was a woman with some fashion sense…and Worf's counterpart brushed after every meal.

A refreshing change, if I do say so myself.

The two Sulus have one characteristic in common—a fascination with pointy objects.

THE GALAXY'S
LEAST
INTERESTING
ALTERNATE REALITY

The one where Riker commands the *Enterprise*. Need I say more?

Oh, the horror!

Robbie Robinson

THE GALAXY'S
LONGEST
CONTINUOUS
WAR

War being the popular thing it is, there are lots of contenders for this title.

Prominent among them is the armed conflict between the Ennis and Nol-Ennis factions of a world in the Gamma Quadrant. At one point, the Ennis and the Nol-Ennis seemed so bent on reducing each other to subatomic particles, the leaders of their planet exiled both gangs to a nearby moon.

A defensive net of artificial satellites was set up to keep out lawyers and insurance salesmen. The planet's leaders also created artificial microbes that repaired any damage to the exiles at a cellular level, ensuring that the combatants would survive no matter how often their livers were pulverized to paste.

The war had already gone on for generations by the time a ship from Deep Space 9 stumbled on it in 2369. You'll be pleased to know that its end is still nowhere in sight.

However, bloody as they are, the Ennis and Nol-Ennis are pikers compared to some of the galaxy's other scrappers....

Let's see...that's Ennis 5,674 to Nol-Ennis 5,670. Yes, you *are* pulling ahead.

Danny Feld

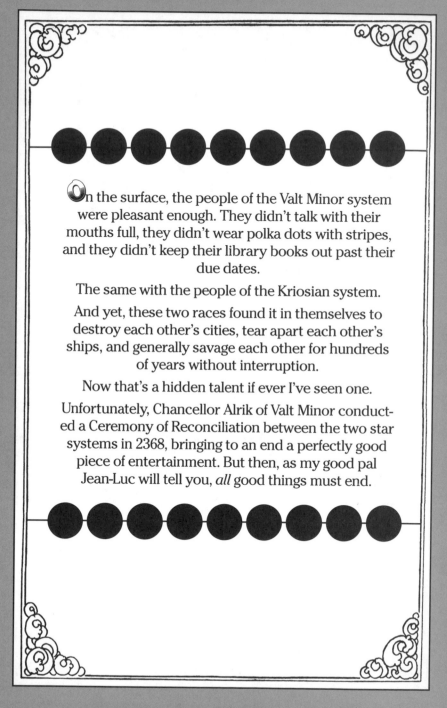

On the surface, the people of the Valt Minor system were pleasant enough. They didn't talk with their mouths full, they didn't wear polka dots with stripes, and they didn't keep their library books out past their due dates.

The same with the people of the Kriosian system.

And yet, these two races found it in themselves to destroy each other's cities, tear apart each other's ships, and generally savage each other for hundreds of years without interruption.

Now that's a hidden talent if ever I've seen one.

Unfortunately, Chancellor Alrik of Valt Minor conducted a Ceremony of Reconciliation between the two star systems in 2368, bringing to an end a perfectly good piece of entertainment. But then, as my good pal Jean-Luc will tell you, *all* good things must end.

Would *you* make peace with this man?

Robbie Robinson

Centuries of enmity and what brings
them together? The drive to wipe out
Starfleet officers. Can't blame them.
I've felt that way myself, once or twice.

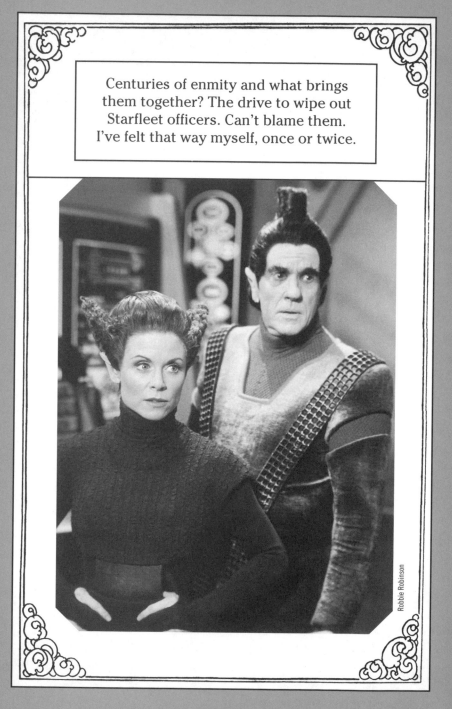

Robbie Robinson

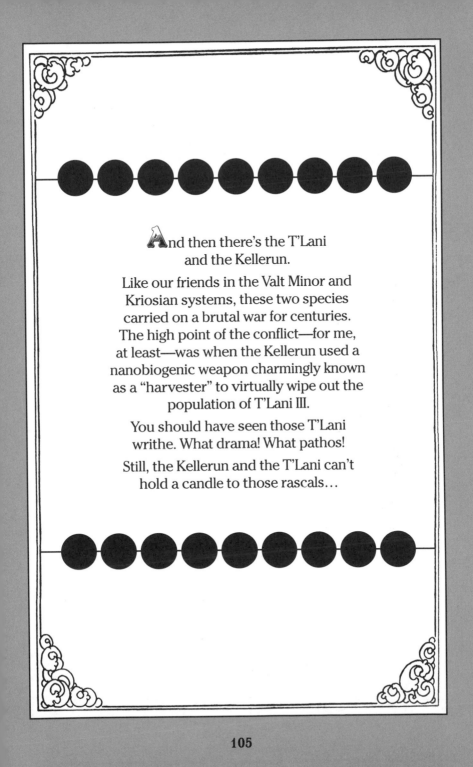

And then there's the T'Lani
and the Kellerun.

Like our friends in the Valt Minor and
Kriosian systems, these two species
carried on a brutal war for centuries.
The high point of the conflict—for me,
at least—was when the Kellerun used a
nanobiogenic weapon charmingly known
as a "harvester" to virtually wipe out the
population of T'Lani III.

You should have seen those T'Lani
writhe. What drama! What pathos!

Still, the Kellerun and the T'Lani can't
hold a candle to those rascals…

...on Eminiar and Vendikar.

Never heard of them? Eminiar VII and Vendikar were worlds at war for a whopping five hundred years. That's half a millennium, if you can wrap your rudimentary mortal consciousnesses around the concept.

And get this—the whole conflict was conducted in a virtual environment. Attacks were launched on a strictly random basis, with any citizens cited as "casualties" willingly reporting to the nearest disintegration station.

Neat. Clean. Elegant. All the heartbreak and cruelty of war without the muss and fuss. Best of all, civilization itself marched on.

That is, until that killjoy Kirk stuck his nose into it. He and his people destroyed Eminiar VII's computers, forcing the two planets to fight their war for real.

Obviously, that wasn't nearly as much fun for either party, so the struggle effectively ended then and there.

The population of the planet Sarpeidon had a small problem. Its sun was on the verge of going nova.

The solution? A novel one. Using a device called the atavachron, everyone on the planet could escape the impending disaster by traveling to an era in Sarpeidon's past.

A fellow named Mr. Atoz, who managed Sarpeidon's vast library, was the one who helped everyone select the appropriate era. It was only when everyone else was gone that Atoz himself escaped—with mere seconds to spare.

And you thought *your* job was stressful.

You'll be glad to learn that Atoz found a place where attractive, half-naked women serve tall, primary-colored drinks with little umbrellas in them. After all, the man deserved it.

The Galaxy's MOST "TIMELY" Evacuation

THE GALAXY'S MEANEST SONUVAGUN

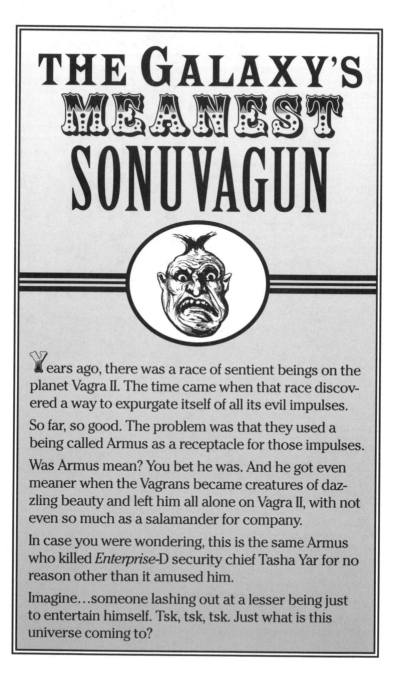

Years ago, there was a race of sentient beings on the planet Vagra II. The time came when that race discovered a way to expurgate itself of all its evil impulses.

So far, so good. The problem was that they used a being called Armus as a receptacle for those impulses.

Was Armus mean? You bet he was. And he got even meaner when the Vagrans became creatures of dazzling beauty and left him all alone on Vagra II, with not even so much as a salamander for company.

In case you were wondering, this is the same Armus who killed *Enterprise*-D security chief Tasha Yar for no reason other than it amused him.

Imagine…someone lashing out at a lesser being just to entertain himself. Tsk, tsk, tsk. Just what is this universe coming to?

Why did it have to be
Yar and not Riker?

The Galaxy's MOST AMBITIOUS USE OF Holographic Technology

In 2340, a clever fellow on Yadera II invented a highly sophisticated hologenerator that created an entire village full of people.

Why? To keep him company, naturally.

This clever fellow—whose name was Rurigan—didn't, even in his wildest dreams, imagine that the village's holographic inhabitants would attain sentience and become legitimate life-forms. But thanks to his hologenerator's advanced software, that's exactly what happened.

Of course, the villagers were still dependent on a machine for their survival. But when you think about it—and I have—so is anyone who travels the galaxy in a silly old starship.

Robbie Robinson

Holographic people...make 'em, trade 'em, collect the whole set.

The Most
ANNOYING
USE OF
HOLOGRAPHIC
TECHNOLOGY

★ ★ ★ ★ ★ ★ ★ ★ ★

No doubt, you've seen this man. Unfortunately, so have I. But unlike Riker he has an off switch.

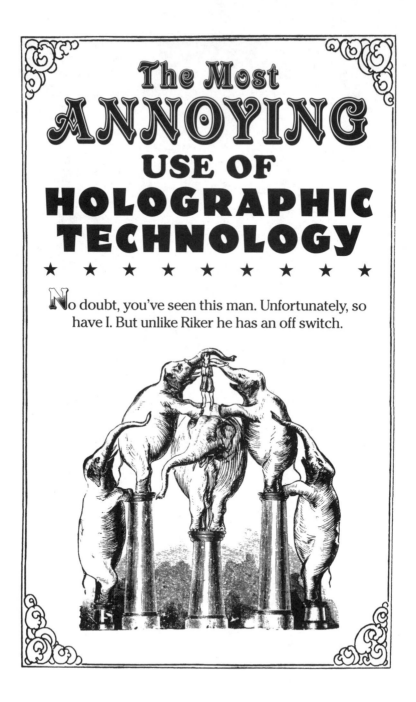

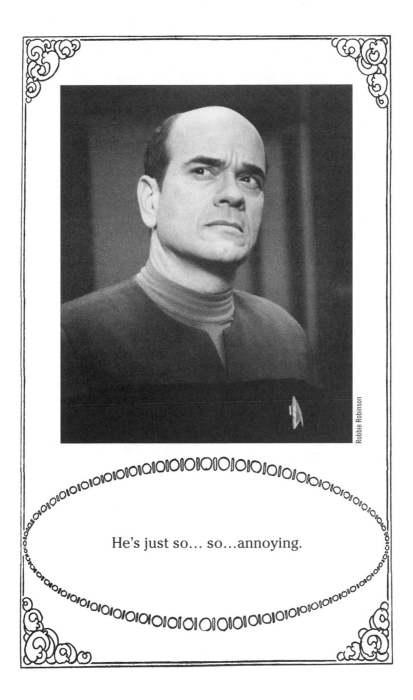

Robbie Robinson

He's just so... so...annoying.

The Galaxy's Most CLEVER CREATION of a TEMPORAL ANOMALY

$\mathcal{F}$ollow me, now.

Imagine an alternate timeline—which we'll call "anti-time"—that flows in the opposite direction from time as you know it. Then imagine an event taking place in the anti-time past.

This event would take on additional significance in the ensuing anti-time present and even more in the anti-time future. But because anti-time flows in the opposite direction from "normal" time, that event would first correspond to your universe's future and become incrementally more significant as it approached your past. (Now *that's* technobabble!)

In this case, we're talking about a temporal anomaly in the Devron system that first presented itself in 2395, then in 2370, and finally in 2364. Starships from these three different eras scanned this anomaly with inverse tachyon beams, bless their cute little deflector dishes.

But what the captains of these vessels didn't realize…is that the beams themselves created and amplified this anomaly, which would eventually grow so mighty as to destroy the very fabric of normal time. Oh, and also life as you know it.

In other words, the anomaly represented a temporal paradox—a puzzle—which I created for *mon bon ami* Jean-Luc Picard. The idea was to give him a chance to prove his intellectual worth and that of his species.

Luckily for you, Jean-Luc solved the puzzle.

This time.

Time and tide wait for no man,
not even—Jean-Luc Picard.

THE GALAXY'S MOST ANNOYING MOURNING RITUAL

The Bajorans mourn their dead with a chant that lasts for two hours—enough to make you wish it had been you who died instead.

The Talarians are even more insane. When one of them prances off their mortal coil, the survivors take part in the *B'Nar*— a rhythmic, high-pitched wail known to attract small rodents, expressed for several hours at a time.

But the Klingons are the worst of all. When one of them bites the proverbial dust, they pry his or her eyes open, then let loose with the most horrific howl you've ever heard.

They say it's a warning to the previously deceased, to let them know a warrior is arriving among them. Seems to me a card would work just as well.

You *could* just send flowers!

117

The Galaxy's MOST IMPRESSIVE Formerly Corporeal ENTITY

Mind you, the planet Meridian, discovered by Benjamin Sisko and his people, is out of the running. After all, it's only "formerly corporeal" part of the time.

But that still leaves a small army of other contenders for the title. Take "John Doe," for instance—a Zalkonian discovered by the *Enterprise*-D in a crashed escape pod in 2366.

"Doe"—given the name by a googly-eyed Beverly Crusher—astounded the doctor and her staff with his rapid recovery from his injuries. (On the other hand, Crusher astounds rather easily. Even Picard seems to impress her.)

Doe was later found to be a member of a persecuted minority in Zalkonian society—a group undergoing a metamorphosis from humanoid form into a noncorporeal one. But if all Doe's cohorts were as wimpy as he was, they probably weren't persecuted *enough*.

Major yawn. Next candidate.

At least she didn't name him *Wesley* Doe.

Robbie Robinson

119

On the planet Zetar, all corporeal life was destroyed thousands of years ago. However, the Zetarians managed to survive in noncorporeal form.

One day, they thought, ohmigosh...what have we done to ourselves? We've got no bodies (which, for the untutored, is basically what noncorporeality is all about).

They then roamed around space for a ridiculously long time, searching for a body in which they could experience the material universe again.

The Zetarians thought they had found such a body when they encountered *Enterprise* crew member Mira Romaine in 2269. But as it turned out, ship's engineer Montgomery Scott was after Romaine's corporeal form as well.

The Zetarians had taken millennia to find a warm mammal. Scott, on the other hand, could build a starship in 3.7 seconds. Guess who won?

Now let's review our third entry...

Some five hundred thousand years ago, a star-spanning civilization devastated itself in a horrific war. Those of its leaders who survived looked around and decided it was time to bury the hatchet.

Good thinking, wasn't it? Of course, if this had occurred to them a bit earlier, they might have preserved the billions of beings who comprised the vast majority of their species. Oh well.

In any case, the war had poisoned their homeworld with radiation, so even these survivors were on the endangered mammals list. But they didn't want to die like everyone else. (Who does?)

So they found a way to distill their consciousnesses out of their bodies and store them like fruit preserves in survival canisters. The idea was for them to be revived after the radiation had gone away—at which time they could go about finding bodies again. Three of them outlasted the expiration date on the canisters—Sargon, Thalassa, and Henoch.

And they found some bodies, all right—in the form of Jim Kirk and two of his officers. However, things didn't quite work out. Sargon and Thalassa ended up drifting into space, Henoch went the way of most ill-mannered noncorporeal types—poof, all gone—and Kirk's corpus had to put up with his mind again.

Was it all an elaborate
ploy to get away from
that annoying Talaxian?

And then there's Kes—an Ocampa who worked in sickbay on Kathy Janeway's ship. Kes had had telepathic abilities for as long as she could remember (a year, at least).

Then Kes made mind-contact with a malevolent Delta Quadrant race (ooh, scary) and her powers started growing exponentially.

In fact, she began affecting the very fabric of matter on the ship—not such a terrible thing, really, when you consider how badly it needed redecorating.

Kathy got rid of the little pest just in time to watch her trash a perfectly good shuttle (Just how many of them do they have?)—and achieve a blissfully noncorporeal state of being. Lullaby, good night, and good riddance.

But for my money, the most imposing example of a formerly corporeal entity...

...As the species known as the Organians—who, when Captain Kirk met them in 2267, appeared to be a simple, agrarian people.

As far as Kirk could tell, the Organians had made no scientific or technological strides in tens of thousands of years. They had no microwave ovens, no video games...and if you asked to borrow their cell phones, they looked at you funny.

In reality, the Organians were advanced life-forms who had developed beyond the need for physical bodies millions of years earlier. When Klingon forces tried to occupy Organia for the planet's strategic value, the Organians rejected them—and their Federation "rescuers" as well.

Then the Organians put the pedal to the metal and imposed the infamous Organian Peace Treaty, which said the Organians would tolerate no hostilities between the Federation and the Klingon Empire. None at all. *Nada*.

You've got to love anyone who sends both the Klingons and the Federation packing. Now, if the Organians had spurned the Romulans and the Cardassians in the bargain, they would have *really* earned some brownie points.

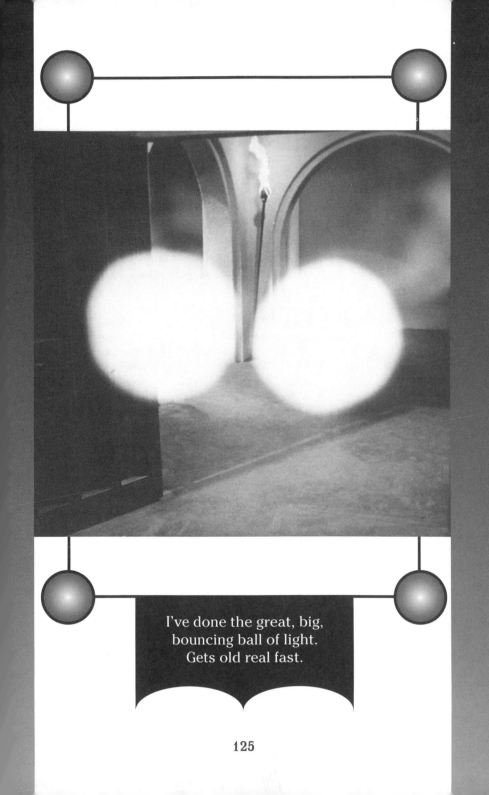

I've done the great, big,
bouncing ball of light.
Gets old real fast.

The Galaxy's
LARGEST PERMANENT
WORMHOLE

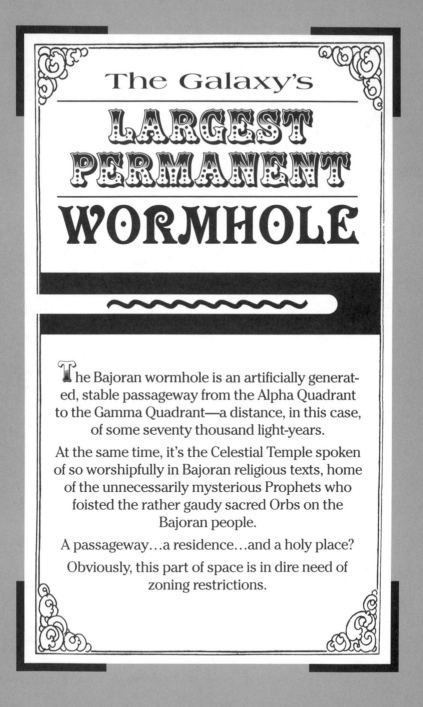

The Bajoran wormhole is an artificially generated, stable passageway from the Alpha Quadrant to the Gamma Quadrant—a distance, in this case, of some seventy thousand light-years.

At the same time, it's the Celestial Temple spoken of so worshipfully in Bajoran religious texts, home of the unnecessarily mysterious Prophets who foisted the rather gaudy sacred Orbs on the Bajoran people.

A passageway…a residence…and a holy place?

Obviously, this part of space is in dire need of zoning restrictions.

An extraordinarily tasteless
phenomenon if you ask me...but
the "Prophets" call it home.

THE LONGEST TIME

RULED BY A

COMPUTER

For centuries, the Fabrini people coasted through space on their way to a promised land—unaware that their world was actually the inside of a big, scooped-out rock.

And what was it that pulled the proverbial wool over their eyes? A clever computer called the Oracle, which masqueraded in their midst as a religious edifice.

Sounds like fun, eh? Some day I'll have to hollow out a casaba melon and put a civilization inside—just to see how it feels.

Of course, the Oracle's regime was a mere drop in the bucket compared to our next candidate.

Some six thousand years ago, the inhabitants of Beta III had a technologically advanced but war-ridden society (hey, it's tough all over). Then a leader named Landru united his people by returning them to a simpler time.

"Hey, you," he said, "put down that thingamajig and go have a picnic. Make lunch, not war." Or something to that effect.

After his death (the result of excessive picnicking), Landru's work was continued by a computer system. (Uh oh—irony alert. It took a computer—a manifestation of technology—to preserve a technology-free society? Hello-o?)

There was definitely trouble in the offing. As I often say, "Never send a bucket of chips and circuits to do an organic being's work."

In this case, the computer interpreted Landru's philosophies a bit too literally, creating a hideously oppressive society with absolutely no individual freedoms. Bad computer, bad…

But if you think six thousand years is a long time to kowtow to a glorified adding machine, consider the case of…

...The Aldeans. For centuries, their world was governed by a sophisticated computer system called The Custodian.

(Actually, I believe its name was Fred. "The Custodian" was its professional name.)

The Custodian was built and programmed by Aldea's Progenitors, a really nice bunch of guys whose identities (and somewhat suspicious bank statements) have since been lost in the mists of time. The system's job was to supply all the needs of Aldea's citizens, freeing them to pursue idyllic lives of artistic creation.

The Custodian also maintained a cloaking device around the planet, which made the Aldeans sterile and therefore incapable of pursuing one *particular* form of artistic creation.

But then, nobody's perfect.
(Except me, of course.)

THE BIGGEST FAVOR

EVER EXTENDED
to a Planetary Population

In 2366, a certain omnipotent and extraordinarily clever being (who shall modestly go unnamed) used his powers to save the inhabitants of Bre'el IV from certain death.

A short time earlier, the passage of a black hole through the Bre'el star system had disrupted the orbit of Bre'el IV's moon. As you can imagine, this posed a major threat to the locals.

And then came…er, that certain omnipotent and extraordinarily clever being. A snap of his fingers and that moon was back where it belonged, gently ruling the tides and inspiring poetry.

Touching, isn't it?

EVER EXTENDED *to the* Entire Federation

THE BIGGEST FAVOR

In 2365, a certain omnipotent and extraordinarily clever being—yes, the same one—transported the *Enterprise*-D some seven thousand light-years beyond Federation space to System J-25. That's where Jean-Luc and his band of bunglers first made contact with the always entertaining Borg.

Without that warning, without firsthand knowledge of what it was up against, the Federation would never have survived the Borg invasion of 2366. I'd say the Federation owes me…I mean, owes that omnipotent being…a debt of gratitude.

Wouldn't you?

If you can excuse their droning,
they make amusing party guests.

THE GALAXY'S MOST BORING EPIC

*T*he *Never Ending Sacrifice* is a Cardassian novel in which several generations of characters lead selfless lives of duty and obedience to the state. It's considered the finest epic in all of Cardassian literature.

The key phrase here is "never ending." This thing is so boring it may actually be deadly to certain species.

To a Q, an entire mortal lifetime seems like the merest blink of an eye—and *still* this thing seems to go on forever.

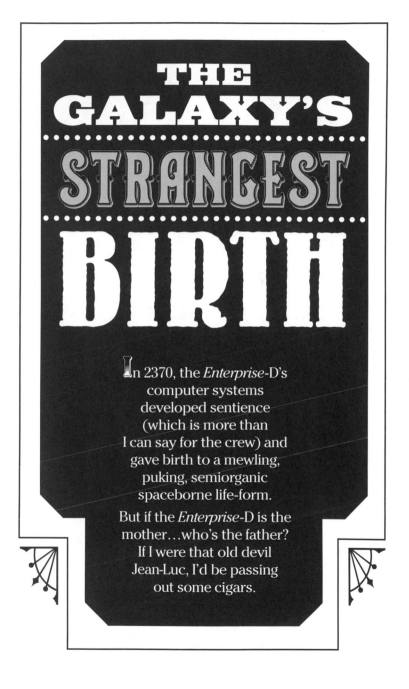

THE GALAXY'S
STRANGEST
BIRTH

In 2370, the *Enterprise*-D's
computer systems
developed sentience
(which is more than
I can say for the crew) and
gave birth to a mewling,
puking, semiorganic
spaceborne life-form.

But if the *Enterprise*-D is the
mother…who's the father?
If I were that old devil
Jean-Luc, I'd be passing
out some cigars.

The Galaxy's
MOST OVERRATED
Source of Inspiration

What is it with this Shakespeare character, anyway? The old Earth hack wrote a few clumsy stage dramas way back in the sixteenth and seventeenth centuries and people are still quoting him eight hundred years later.

And it's not just Earthmen. In the twenty-third century, that Klingon blowhard General Chang was a big fan of Shakespeare's works as well.

Almost a hundred years later, Picard keeps a leather-bound copy of Shakespeare's plays in his ready room…and Data's skipping about as Prospero and Henry V in the holodeck.

I must say, I don't see the attraction. Come on, folks. The old sot is dead and buried. Get over it. Move on.

A mechanical man playing Henry V?
Must be a sign of the apocalypse.

The
LONGEST-LIVED
BEINGS
in the
UNIVERSE

(Other than the Q, of course.)

Well, let's see. There are the
El-Aurians…You-Know-Who's people.

In fact, You-Know-Who herself is five hundred years
old if she's a day, and by El-Aurian standards she's
not even middle-aged. That means she could
go on another…

…thousand years?

Pardon me. I think I'm going to be ill.

Is it *just* the good supposed
to die *young?*

$\mathbb{T}$hen there's Flint,
who was born in Mesopotamia in
3834 B.C. Flint enjoyed a unique talent
for instant tissue regeneration, which time
and again enabled him to survive disease, war, and
the wrath of jealous husbands.

Though we'll never know for sure,
I think he might even have survived
Neelix's casseroles.

To conceal his longevity from his fellow man,
Flint lived in a great many places, always
pretending to age (probably, by hunching
over and hawking up phlegm) and then
moving on.

During his lifetime, his identities included some of
mankind's most influential figures, including
Alexander the Great, Johannes Brahms, and the
guy who invented game shows—easily *the* most
annoying thing humans have come up with.

When Flint finally bought the farm, as a result of
having left Earth's beneficial environs, he was more
than six thousand years old—though he didn't
look a day over 5,600.

I remember this human…
arrogant, self-serving, vain, petty,
aggressive. But then, that really
describes them all.

When it comes to long lives, I should also mention the inhabitants of Gamma Trianguli VI, who had a life expectancy of about ten thousand years—until the crew of the original *Enterprise* came along and upset the applecart.

On the other hand, Kirk's interference made the Gamma Triangulans a lot more interested in procreation, so maybe it wasn't such a bad deal after all.

A whole
new outlook
for the
cosmetically
challenged.

But the universe's truly longest-lived beings would be Bele and Lokai, last survivors of the "civilized" planet Cheron. Unaware that racial hatred had reduced their world to a burned-out piece of belly-button lint, Bele pursued Lokai across the galaxy for fifty thousand years until he caught him in 2268.

And they say *I* know how to carry a grudge.

Here's a riddle for you:
"What is black and white, and
chases a 'criminal' all across
the galaxy?"

THE GALAXY'S
QUICKEST
MULTIPLYING
SPECIES

No contest here. Tribbles, a species of small, furry creatures, procreate without pause and enjoy an insanely short gestation period.

However, their rate of reproduction is dependent on their ability to ingest food. So if you've got a houseful of tribbles and you don't know what to do, let the little critters go hungry for a while.

And don't invite any Klingons over for dinner. Tribbles and Klingons do *not* get along.

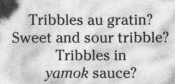

Tribbles au gratin?
Sweet and sour tribble?
Tribbles in
yamok sauce?

The Galaxy's MOST USER-FRIENDLY Space-Time PHENOMENON

Scientifically speaking, the phenomenon known as "the nexus" is a "nonlinear temporal continuum in which reality appears to reshape itself in fulfillment of a person's wishes." In other words, you can have whatever you want...but first you've got to get inside.

The catch is that the gateway to the nexus only crosses your galaxy every thirty-nine years. As luck would have it, two *Enterprise* captains—Jim Kirk and Jean-Luc Picard— have both had occasion to enter the thing and have their dreams served to them on simulated platters.

In Picard's dreamworld, he had a ball and chain and a gang of sniveling brats...that is, a loving wife and four beautiful tykes.

In Kirk's nexus reality, he was living in a condemned cabin with a monstrous canine named Butler and a carton of Ktarian eggs. And he had deluded himself into thinking he would set things right with a woman he had loved—if he could only remember which one.

Of course, both men eventually left the nexus of their own free will...which tells you, once again, that humans don't know a good thing when they see one.

Elliott Marks

Jean-Luc, this is your
ultimate fantasy? You have
got to get out more.

THE GALAXY'S WORST MEALTIME ACCOMPANIMENT

On Marejaretus VI, home of the Ooolans, it's traditional to repeatedly strike two large stones together during a meal. Those present must continue to eat until the stones are broken...

...or until someone grabs them and uses them to beat the striker senseless.

Lieutenant Commander Data of the *Enterprise*-D once said that the Ooolans' stone-smashing ritual reminded him of the chimes rung on Betazed to give thanks for food.

But then, what do you expect from a life-form whose idea of haute cuisine is a semiorganic nutrient suspension in a silicon-based liquid medium?

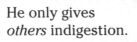

He only gives *others* indigestion.

151

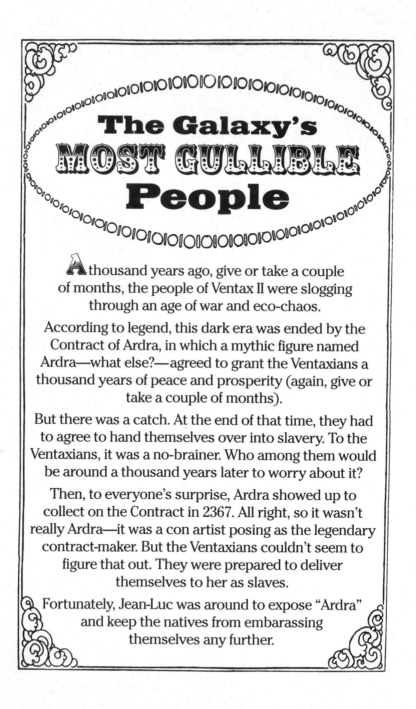

The Galaxy's MOST GULLIBLE People

A thousand years ago, give or take a couple of months, the people of Ventax II were slogging through an age of war and eco-chaos.

According to legend, this dark era was ended by the Contract of Ardra, in which a mythic figure named Ardra—what else?—agreed to grant the Ventaxians a thousand years of peace and prosperity (again, give or take a couple of months).

But there was a catch. At the end of that time, they had to agree to hand themselves over into slavery. To the Ventaxians, it was a no-brainer. Who among them would be around a thousand years later to worry about it?

Then, to everyone's surprise, Ardra showed up to collect on the Contract in 2367. All right, so it wasn't really Ardra—it was a con artist posing as the legendary contract-maker. But the Ventaxians couldn't seem to figure that out. They were prepared to deliver themselves to her as slaves.

Fortunately, Jean-Luc was around to expose "Ardra" and keep the natives from embarassing themselves any further.

Ardra...it's the same forward and
backward. Who said this book
isn't educational?

The Galaxy's
WORST
MASS
MURDERER

The galaxy abounds with bloody pretenders to the title. We'll start with the tamest and work our way up.

First on our list? The Romulan commander who led the assault on the Klingon outpost at Khitomer in 2346.

Some four thousand Klingons were killed in the incident, the only survivors being a Klingon child named Worf (yes, *that* Worf, unfortunately) and his nursemaid, Kahlest.

Years later, it was learned that a Klingon named Ja'rod had betrayed his comrades by giving the Romulans secret defense access codes. Now, I ask you…wasn't that naughty of him?

Next on our little murderer's row is the esteemed Kodos the Executioner, who served as governor of the planet Tarsus IV in 2246. When the colony's food stores were destroyed by a nasty old fungus, Kodos seized power and declared martial law.

Then he rationed the remaining food supply by picking four thousand colonists—or half the population—to be put to death. Marvelous plan, wasn't it?

Then something happened that Kodos hadn't anticipated: A catering vessel arrived with plenty of food for everyone. Unfortunately, only half the colony was still alive to enjoy it. The other half had already been phaser-fried.

It's no wonder that Kodos disappeared afterward. Who wants to be known as a party pooper?

Ever hear of a nifty little race called the Husnock? No? Then here's a primer, containing all you'll ever need to know about them.

1) They were rather violent. In fact, make that *really* violent.

2) In 2366, they descended on the Federation colony at Delta Rana IV, ravaging the planet's surface and killing all but one of the eleven thousand colonists there.

(More on the Husnock later.)

Moving right along, we come to the so-called Crystalline Entity—a spaceborne organism that resembled a big, fluffy snowflake. The entity survived by munching on the energy of other life-forms, judging by the trail of death, devastation, and dental floss it left on planet after planet.

In 2336, the entity destroyed the Omicron Theta colony, where the android you know as Data had been put together. That turned out to be a mistake—because years later, a Dr. Kila Marr, whose son had died at Omicron Theta, shattered the entity with a modulated graviton beam.

S'long, Crystalline Entity.

Dr. Ma'Bor Jetrel is the science whiz who developed that special weapon of annihilation known as the metreon cascade. During the war between the Talaxians and the Haakonians, Jetrel's weapon was used on the Talaxian moon Rinax, resulting in some three hundred thousand Talaxian funerals.

Jetrel later felt guilty about his role in the massacre and spent years searching for a way to make amends. In time, he came up with a regenerative fusion process, with which he hoped to restore some of the dead to life.

It didn't work. It seems Jetrel was a lot better at making people dead than at making them alive again.

After he mastered that egg-in-the-bottle trick, it was only a matter of time until he annihilated an entire planet.

Robbie Robinson

The Borg, one of the galaxy's more fashion-challenged races, came close to wiping out the population of the El-Aurian homeworld in the latter part of the twenty-third century. As it was, the Borg made the El-Aurians' planet a twisted wasteland, spurring the survivors to flee for their lives on the planet's few remaining ships.

One of those survivors was you-know-who—who would come to be known as the bartender on Jean-Luc's flying bucket. It's the one oversight for which I'll never forgive the Borg.

Never.

The blood of millions is on their hands. I ask you...would one more have been so much to ask?

Danny Feld

161

As his first action in the captain's chair, the James T. Kirk of the mirror universe suppressed a Gorlan uprising by pounding an entire rebel planet to dust. His second action was the cold-blooded execution of five thousand colonists on Vega IX.

There's more—but I think you get the idea. Miss Congeniality, he wasn't.

The bodies pile higher and higher, and
yet he keeps that boyish smile.

Nomad was an interstellar probe launched from Earth in 2002. Its mission? To seek out new life and new civilizations, to boldly go—

Whoops. Wrong interstellar probe.

Actually, *Nomad*'s job was simply to scan the void for unknown life-forms. Not a particularly lofty assignment, I'll grant you, but it seems to have paid the bills.

Unfortunately, during its long and otherwise uneventful jaunt through the cosmos, *Nomad* collided with an alien space probe called *Tan Ru*. *Nomad* somehow repaired its widdle boo-boos— but in the process, merged its control programs with those of the other probe.

It's like mixing chocolate and peanut butter— you get something a little different from either component. In this case, you got a single, very deadly probe, its new raison d'être to seek out and sterilize imperfect biological infestations... and believe me, there's no shortage of *those* in the galaxy.

The new and improved *Nomad* destroyed four billion beings in the Malurian system until Jim Kirk tricked it into destroying itself— thereby bringing the death toll to four billion and one.

Take this little fix-it-upper and you can
destroy an entire solar system.

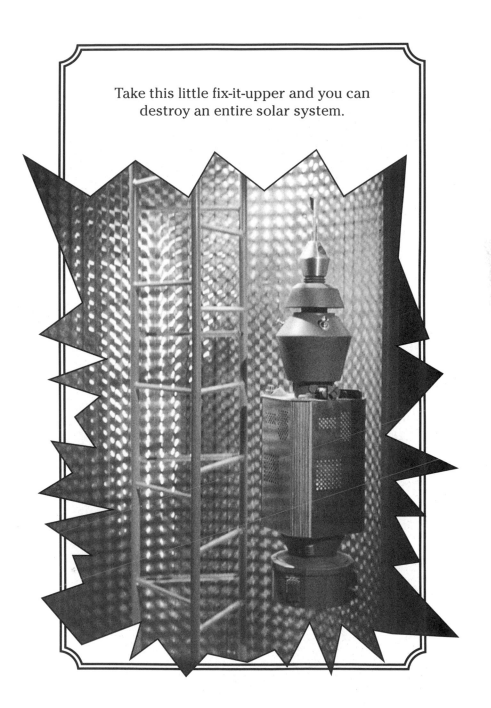

In the twenty-fourth century, the Klingon Empire hunted down and destroyed every tribble it could find, in one of the galaxy's truly spectacular attempts at genocide. The list of small, furry victims ran into the billions.

You see? I told you Klingons didn't like tribbles.

In 2267, an automated space-going weapon from outside your galaxy—a kilometers-long device known only as "the planet killer"—annihilated almost every world in star systems L-370 and L-374. System L-370 alone was home to billions of inhabitants.

I emphasize "was."

The real tragedy is that all the good names for star systems were taken before L-370 got into the act. It's a lot easier to deal with annihilation if your system has a name like Rigel or Aldebaran instead of something out of a cosmic bingo game.

Anyway, the planet killer was destroyed a short time later, when Jim Kirk sent the hulk of a starship into its maw-—and then blew up the starship.

Can you say "Bon appétit?"

Remember the happy-go-lucky Husnock, who rubbed out all but one of the Federation colonists on Delta Rana IV?

As it turns out, that lone survivor was a Douwd—a pretty powerful energy being (even by my standards) who had taken on a human identity and a human wife.

The Douwd loved his wife very much. When the Husnock killed her, the poor fellow was beside himself with grief. In retribution, he destroyed the Husnock.

Not just those who had made the assault on the colony, but every Husnock everywhere.

The *entire* Husnock species.

And they say I have a temper.

The Last
SENTIENT BEINGS
you Want to
INVITE
to a
PARTY

The Nausicaans have earned a reputation for being surly, quick to violence, and having the worst haircuts in the known universe. Just after his graduation from Starfleet Academy, Ensign Jean-Luc Picard had a disagreement with a trio of Nausicaans over a dom-jot game.

One of the Nausicaans ended up backstabbing Picard right through the heart—and he was by far the most levelheaded of the three.

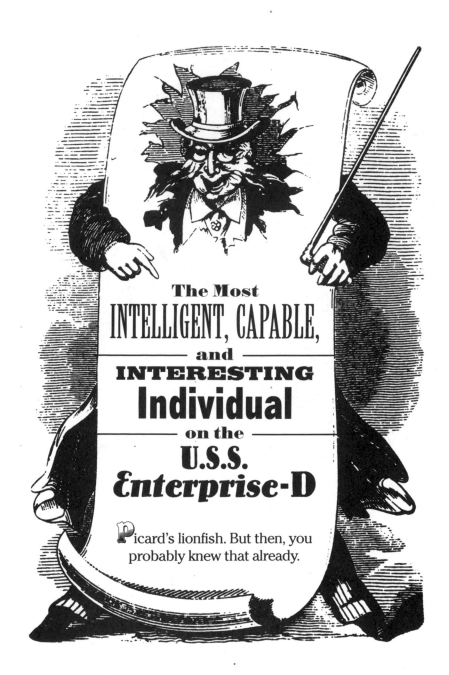

The Most
INTELLIGENT, CAPABLE,
and
INTERESTING
Individual
on the
U.S.S.
Enterprise-D

Picard's lionfish. But then, you probably knew that already.

No real awareness of what
is going on around him—
but then, I should be talking about
the fish and not Picard.